Testimony
by
Donald Carlson

A Poetic Retelling of the Gospel According to
John

Table of Contents

Dedication

This book is dedicated to all of my poetic associates and mentors, especially Dan, Dennis, and Tim; to my friend and teacher John Alvis; but most of all to Anna, my kindest critic, who thinks that this should be a play.

Special thanks to Jae Haeng Rhee for the sublime illustrations both for the cover and the front matter.

Author's Note

Although I consider it best that the poems speak for themselves, I wanted to write a few words to explain both what I am and am not trying to do in this work. I am NOT trying to proselytize or propagate the faith through these poems. Nor did I necessarily create them as an expression of my personal faith, even if they ultimately may be. In writing the poems I set out to explore how powerfully the Gospel stories engage the reader's imagination and how much room they afford for the imagination to move around within them. The old debate is whether salvation comes from faith or works, and it is clear that the Gospels make an appeal both to the mind and to the heart. I am not ready to make the claim that salvation comes from imagination, but its absence makes either the assent of faith or the performing of works that much more difficult. I believe it is the means by which these stories can penetrate the soul.

IN THE BEGINNING

In the Word was the beginning
And the Word contains worlds
That refract on the tongue into torrents of words

Moving deep in the mind of the Father
Who speaks the Word and breathes the world
Into form dimension vibration

Creating the world with the Word
All of it--elephant tusk dog tongue and antennae
Coral reef tree trunk neutron and nebulae

Uttering a before and an after
Uttering a fire of love song and breath
Uttering history and memory through the Word

Who became of a piece with the world
Filling the flesh of this world with himself
A Son to dwell with us and bring us the light

Not the light of the burning lantern
Or the light of a candle or of galaxies
But himself the Light come to light among us

And his own refused to own him
The Word entering the world to relight it
For they knew and preferred the darkness

He had come to refather an orphaned world
Placing the Father's name on our tongues
In an acceptable time--the time ordained for testimony

JOHN THE BAPTIST

I am not the one.
How many times do I have to tell them that
Before they believe me?

I may act the part
Dressed in camel skins
And famous for my penitential practices

Locusts and honey
Are not the delicacies Scribes and Pharisees
Keep on their tables.

I accuse them to their faces
Of their crimes--the vipers preying on the people
Cry out for their repentance

And there are baptisms
The washing off in the river's murky stream of their sins
Their carapace of vices

I keep telling them
I am here for only one thing to be the voice that says
Make straight!

None of it is about me
I would diminish fade away
If only they will let me

ANDREW

You may think of me as a lead actor in a minor role
A bit player who only functions
To get the major action off and rolling

With a cameo or two along the way.
My big moment seems to happen early on
But pay more respect to the story please

And you may come to see me in a different light.
I was the Go-Between the one who always paid attention
To where the plot was heading quietly awaiting my cue to speak up

Or act as the moment required to get business done.
You may think it was Simon or the Beloved One
Who were the foremost but I. . . I made

That important introduction to my brother Simon
On the cloudless day near the olive drab currents
Of the Jordan the day after John sent me and an unnamed other

Following the one he called Lamb of God.
And months after in that cool mountain meadow covered
In an emerald carpet with the famished masses

I called his attention to the lad with loaves and fish
With which he fed five thousand thus stoking the drama
When the multitude got it wrong because he'd filled

Each one's belly--their idol and one perennial lord.
No without my subtle influence at just the right moments
The Lamb would never have been led to slaughter
Or mapped out for me the pattern of my own diagonal death

NATHANAEL

He called me Israelite True Blue
A dig at me on account of my caustic remark
To Philip about Nazareth no doubt

As if anything good had ever come from that lowlife
Town full of charlatans whose dusty streets are home
To scavenging dogs and flies

The story makes you think he won me with that parlor trick
Of telling me he saw me sitting beneath the fig tree
Before Philip even came to me

True enough he caught me off guard
But it was less the vision and the marvel
That won me than the thrill of being called

Did I see the heavens opened and angels
Ascending and descending on the Son of Man
As I was promised you may ask?

That's for me to know but I assure you
That I did see something as wondrous.
I saw the death called love

MARY HIS MOTHER

If you think it was easy
Being his mother think again.
Of course he was different

Yet he wasn't a prodigy
Not in the usual sense
No precious boyhood tricks

Reviving dead sparrows
Nothing of that sort
Contrary to what you may think

He wasn't a mother's boy. I remember
One spring with cotton drifting
From the willows of the wadi

How he insisted on staying
In the synagogue long into the night
Disputing fine points of the Law with the rabbis

Though he was barely a teenager
And his brethren taunted him with being
A know-it-all--a loser--as if he cared.

Not that he kept aloof--he played
With other children--he roved the town
Exploring inventing new games for them

I don't know that anyone could say
How all this would lead us to the moment
On the hilltop seeing him both emptied and exalted

As I stared up at him and he looked down
At me with agony covering his face the hardest
Thing was seeing myself reflected in his eyes

THE STEWARD

Did they have any idea
What foolishness this was?
These two youngsters
Thinking they could make
A life of meagerness together
In this godforsaken country?

When the ceremony started
Among the stone huts the sun was broiling
Its harsh light falling on the twisted trees
That grow in our shallow rocky soil
Yet things cooled as the sun sank into the sea
Merriment began to spread through the place
As musicians played pipes and drums
And some of the feasters tipsy now
Joined the snaking swirling dance

Just then the table servants discovered
That the wine had failed
As they were puzzling out what to do
To salvage something of this unspooling day

The servants saw his mother lean toward him
And say something softly in his ear
Then saw him draw back and reply
With a stern look that made them wonder
But when she held her ground they knew she'd won
Then she motioned to them and they obeyed
As if she'd been herself the mother of the bridegroom

I was to say the least astonished
Later I learned the whole story
But then I was confused
Thought that the groom
Had played a trick saving the best for last
Waiting late into the feast
To serve the most exquisite wine.

As I congratulated the bridegroom
My heart grew light too
When I saw him blushing intoxicated
With the wine of his surprise

NICODEMUS

I had come with only one servant to carry a torch
Not the entourage with horns to announce my approach
The usual way for us Pharisees.

It was a moonless night the air close
Shadow begetting shadow the torch light absorbed
As if by black velvet layered in folds on the street

The quarter of town where he stayed was not the one
We Pharisees frequented seedy disreputable even
The quarter crowded with sinners whose houses

Were dwellings of defilement I felt pollution
Beset me as the edges of a parchment scroll
Are beset by mice who can find nothing else to nibble

When he invited me into the dwelling
I had reservations thought twice about staying
Began to make excuses about leaving right away

The smoke from the oil lamps was smudging
The plastered wall so that what was once creamy
Had turned dirty and brown but I stayed in spite of myself

Whatever power of his had brought me there
Held me now and would not let me leave.
In return for my gushing affirmation of belief

He offered a riddle that almost put me off
The whole shabby affair of being his follower
The suggestion smacked faintly of something queer.

I tried to turn it into a jest
But couldn't quite pull it off shocked as I was
By the hint of impurity the absurdity

Of being carried in mother's womb a second time

After living my long life fastidiously in avoidance of filth
And ritual uncleanness such as that which attaches to childbirth.

But now? Now somehow all is changed
Now I hunger to be born again.
It's precisely as easy and hard as you think

THE SAMARITAN WOMAN

As I bantered with him
Prodding him with quips about his people
His eyes drilled down into the thirsty core of me

What could he possibly want from me?

It was more than water I could tell.

The dust of the road was all over him
As he leaned wearily against the well
I could see that he'd walked a long way
To get here the middle of nowhere
The heart of enemy territory my home
The home of a crude proud needy race

The midafternoon sun was enough
To drain the heart from anyone
Who'd been walking in it

It was reddening my skin
The water jar chafing the shoulder
Where I carried it

When he spoke of living water
I wondered if the sun had softened his brain
This Jewish wanderer or whether
He was toying with me as all men did
Finding me an easy target for their scorn
An easy mark for their desires

Then he proceeded to haul my secrets out of me
He was draining from my well the brackish water
That ran too bitter to do myself
Or anyone else much good

THE OFFICIAL FROM CAPERNAUM

How does one know that one
Has experienced a miracle? That
Question never troubled me until now

As I look back on my boy's illness
Each remedy applied failing
The gradual fading of his life's breath

The looming of desperation of one
Hope left kept alive by mere rumor
Of his works and whispers that he was the one

And that he was headed this way
Back to his own country after the feast.
The talk of his singular behavior in the Temple.

There was no time to sort out whether
He was merely a charlatan or truly a prophet
My boy would be gone soon it would be too late.

When I met him in the road tired and hot dust
Devils swirling I faltered thinking I had made
A mistake his apparent irritation putting me off

Yet I worked up the courage and asked
Thinking I had nothing really to lose having
Already stripped myself of dignity just by being there.

His vexation at my asking made me feel smaller but
Then a change something like resignation or pity
Came over his face and he gave me his word.

At that moment I felt myself and my son lifted
Above any doubt I turned transformed at the seventh
Hour knowing that indeed I already had my miracle

THE LAME MAN

Waiting was life and life was waiting
Waiting for the stirring in the water
Waiting to move myself into the pool
Waiting while the others went before me
Waiting for the cycle to repeat itself

Year after year of waiting daily
In the portico of the pool near Sheep Gate
Even on the Sabbath I never rested from waiting

And so that still Sabbath morning I was lying
As usual on my pallet trying to bestir myself
When the mob began moving as whatever
Power it was that moved the water divinely
Started to ripple and swirl its slate gray surface
Cut off frustrated again by the crowd
Stepping and plunging into the pool
On their own or with the help of friends.

When he crossed into my light and stood over me
He asked what was I waiting for

PHILIP

I hope it's not bragging to say
First he found me then I became a channel
Through which others came to him.

Although that evokes a metaphor he
Didn't use as prominently as others.
He seemed more fond of the pastoral--

Sheep and shepherds vines and branches.
But those who came to him through me sought
With the eyeless hunger of water that never knows

Exactly what it seeks just flows
Ceaselessly moving toward a place
Of rest where it can pool and grow until

Before you know it pool becomes
Pond becomes lake becomes sea
Nurturing an understory of living creatures.

When he asked me where to find food
To feed the multitude I gave him the wrong
Answer but it was the answer he wanted

Something dull and common--foil to make
The jewel of his miracle sparkle the more.
Then there was my own eyeless request

After our supper that he show us the Father
As if I hadn't seen all along what he was doing
But it's fine to play the fool when the love's that sharp

THE LAD WITH LOAVES AND FISH

What was I doing out in the middle of nowhere
A mere child with a cargo of five loaves and two fish
A very long way from the place we call home?

Some would say my parents wouldn't have set
Out across the lake empty handed to follow him
We knew not where for who knows how long

That always thinking ahead just before boarding the boat
Mother ran back home and packed the loaves and fish in a basket
Putting me in charge like a big boy giving me something to do. Fools.

Whoever said I was linked to that multitude?
My parents were nowhere to be found as if such as I have
Human parents at least in the usual sense

No I was there to fulfill a destiny embedded among the hungry crowd
In its trek across the choppy waters in search of wonders
In that distant emerald field remote from any town.

Did you ever think to ask why the number off my loaves and fish
Add up to seven? Or the baskets of leftovers gathered to twelve?
How do you think I found my way into this story anyway?

THE MULTITUDE

He gave us bread when we were hungry
On that sunny emerald hillside where we sat munching
We would have crowned him king then and there

But then he took away that bread
Leaving us with hard sayings and puzzlement
In its place nothing to munch on but hot air

He had us again after Lazarus and we covered the dusty
Road into Jerusalem with palm branches and cloaks
While he rode through the heat haze amidst our hosannas

But instead of triumphs there were troubled looks
More confusion his brow creased with foreboding
A rumble from the sky like thunder some said it was the voice of God

Finally he stood before us in Pilate's courtyard
Wearing a crown plaited from a tree of thorns
While we called out Crucify him! with everything we had

THE BRETHREN

He was always getting in the way always
Underfoot almost from the moment he was born
Running around in Joseph's shop with his nose running

As soon as he could talk his mouth ran too
Never stopped running with baby talk and then
With precocious nonsense that everyone thought was darling

Some would simply call our feelings sibling rivalry
Others would chalk it up to jealousy--Rubbish!
How would you feel if someone you knew

As an infant unable to do anything for himself starts
To be called prophet Messiah even with miracles
Credited to his name? Hard to fathom

Even harder to swallow we looked for ways to trip him up
Trying to send him at the Tabernacles into the hands
Of his enemies but he outmaneuvered us as usual.

However this isn't what you really want to know
It's how we came to be known as his brethren.
Were we sons of Mary and Joseph or cousins

Or Joseph's children from a previous union?
Again we'll cut through those idle questions.
We are who we are--your twins your doppelganger

THE PHARISEES

No way were we going to let that snipe
That false prophet that blasphemer from Nazareth
Get away with toppling our sect

Rather we would dog his every step
Looking for any excuse to take him down
Casting our shadow upon anyone

Whose life he may have touched with his provocations
His clear defiance of the regulations
Laid down by Moses in the Law

Some say that we appear in the account
To smear culpability for his rejection and bloodguilt
For his death on the Jews our people

Perhaps there is something to that
In fact the reflection in our glass throws
Back a multitude of faces some Jewish many not

That's no concern of ours the one and only thing
We would have you know is that in our finest moment
We proclaimed Caesar to be our only king

THE WOMAN TAKEN

I couldn't even read
No one had taught me
Yet even I could see that whatever
He was tracing on the ground
In that familiar yet undecipherable alphabet
Was sending thrills and shocks of scandal
And embarrassment through the crowd

When they were all gone
The stones that they had dropped
With which they meant to break the body
That I had defiled by contact with that other
Were scattered all around the temple court
And he refused to condemn me
Told me I could go

The day was cooling past its prime
A little wind blew up small swirls of dust
The only sound was the constant call and answer
The hollow hooting of gray doves
Roosting in the olive trees

I turned away and walked toward my home
Nothing seemed changed but
My soul had been bruised indelibly
By the stones of his love

THE MAN BORN BLIND

My birth was not an auspicious one
A burden and a curse to my poor parents
The outward sign of what their neighbors labelled their infamy

For what dark blasphemy what sacrilege
Had I been inflicted upon them or was I the abomination
Myself some braid of evil twisted into flesh in mother's womb?

The sun fell on my face as I sat in my usual spot
Just outside the Temple gate waiting for a drizzle of coins
To plink onto the cloak spread out before me

A burble of human noises passed back and forth
Around me on the road sparking my hopes that today
Would yield enough coin to buy tomorrow's bread.

I could sense someone passing me
Whose passing itself had something of the breeze in it
We spoke he stooped I heard him spitting and thought it mockery

Till I sensed the swishing of his fingers in soil felt
The strange warmth of dirt and spittle traced over my eyes
Heard groaning in his voice when he said Go wash.

When my eyes first found the light
A different kind of darkness overtook me for a moment
A rush of joy I could hardly believe or contain

If you had told me then that with sight would come
Such trouble I would have laughed at you
But before I knew it the Pharisees were there grilling me

Relentless after the marvel of my healing
They stubbornly kept asking the wrong questions
As if their stone eyes couldn't see the right ones to ask

THOMAS

You may be inclined to call me Doubter
Or that other nettling epithet The Twin
Take a moment's pause to think please before you call me either

Both have hardened into handy cliche
But there are other moments in my story
From which I would have you make additions to my name.

When he decided against all common sense
To abandon his safe haven across the Jordan
After hearing of Lazarus' plight it was my defining moment.

Let's go and die with him I told the others
Feeling resolute and clear-eyed as I ever had
In all my days knowing what I stood for was worth

Laying down life for or so I thought.
The hilly country where we were lying low was
Of no interest to the self-anointed guardians of the Law.

Nor did that little hill town where we took refuge
Interest our band--foot soldiers of the new dispensation.
So yes I was ready for death. I wasn't prepared for word of love's
triumph

LAZARUS

I would have liked to have told him
What my sisters told him but since they'd
Already said it what would be the point?
Besides I didn't want to seem ungrateful
It was no small thing that he did
And my sisters told me that he wept
That was in fact the first thing that I noticed
When they'd loosed me from the sudarium
That his eyes were red

When I heard his voice as if through water
I was in the middle of a nightmare
The mordant fires of Gehenna casting
Darkness all around instead of light
There was howling and loud screeches
Dry and unhinged as cicadas shrieking

When I came to myself in my own body
I caught for a moment an acrid stench
Masked by the aroma of myrrh and aloes
And the nard with which sister Mary
Had anointed me that lingered then left

When I saw daylight flooding that cave
I barely made it off the slab without falling
My hands and legs still bound by the burial cloths
I was like a sheep tied up for shearing

That was some weeks ago
My sisters still fawn over me
Wait on me hand and foot
Still in disbelief that I am back
I too of course can hardly believe it
Yet something gnaws at my rejoicing

Revived have I been made clean again
Or since I have lain in those cerements
And caught the whiff of my own corruption
Will I forever be defiled?

And he?
At first he played it cautious for awhile
He now has gone to Jerusalem where powerful
Enemies wait for the time to spring their traps
Rumors float abroad that they also want me dead

If they come they'll find me lying here at table
Calmly drinking from my alabaster cup

MARTHA

When my brother began to waste
Away I wasn't worried in the least.
Although I knew that the teacher had gone

Because he had fanned the anger
Against him to a white heat I knew
That he wouldn't let the friend he loved so well

Succumb to something as common
As fever when he had healed so many
Of illnesses far worse perfect strangers to boot

And we were so much more to him
Than strangers closer than family
More than disciples my sister my brother and I

Ours was a fellowship of heart mind
Spirit that I never imagined could be
Broken by time or distance or even by death

Which made the slap of his silence
Far more stinging when he didn't come
Leaving our brother Lazarus to dwindle and die.

When he finally arrived four days
Too late once we got over the pure shock
Of his late appearance the sense of a rupture never

To be healed there was only one word
In our hearts and on our lips--If he had only been here--
Both a confession and a rebuke searing as an open wound

Yet he behaved as if nothing was different when
He led us to the tomb tears starting to fall a groan in his breath
Wiping my hands on my apron I warned him there'd be a stench

Brushing me aside he inhaled and with that intake
Of breath it was as if it were the first breath ever to be drawn
Restoring all as he released it and cried out Lazarus, arise

CAIAPHAS

Sitting together long into the night
The torches guttering debating irresolute with Lazarus raised
The crowd soon would be waving him with palm branches into the
city

It was all I could do to endure the others looking
Indecisive playing nervously with the fringes of their tallits
Their heads filled with confusion phylacteries moving side-to-side

Only I among them knew how things had to be done
Being powerful myself I knew firsthand the loyalty
Or should I say the treachery of members of an inner circle

I knew one of his own would turn and seek us out
No need to go after him among the crowd
We would take him quietly in some out-of-the-way place

Turn his own words against him double-edged
Let our agenda justify whatever means it took
Don't you think I knew what I was doing that I knew what was at
stake?

Disciple of the Law as I am
Did you truly think there was any veiled meaning
When I said it is better that one man should die for the nation?

JUDAS ISCARIOT

I'm not asking for your sympathy
Not that you'd give it to me anyway.
My double entry bookkeeping

As keeper of the money box
Put me in control of all accounts
Of what came in and what went out.

With all the funds thus given to my care
You'd have thought he'd keep a closer eye on me
But he treated all I treasured as so much trash.

Yet my legend grew as it was bound to
You can't ignore the purchase of my infamy
I have won for myself something of a following.

The Gospel says I sided with the devil
That the devil entered me as I swallowed
The savory morsel he dipped into the dish

Whether anyone would buy that in this enlightened
Age is open to question let's just say that between
His total disregard for the silvery ring of a Roman coin

And his constant sniping at the powerful
Who can always crush a threat I snapped.
I never should have trusted him in the first place

MALCHUS

It's not as if I had any choice in the matter
The temple guard and other servants grabbed me
And pulled me from my warm covers
Shivering--such a cold night--
Shoved a torch in my hand
And pushed me along with the mob
Sent out to seize someone they called "The Teacher"
Although they said it sarcastically enough
A troublemaker they said with one of his sometime followers
Leading us out to a garden on the side of the mountain

When we'd found him there was
Some movement and some talk--
I could barely see beyond my torch light
When suddenly someone swung something
Then the burning the blood on the right side of my face
Disfiguring, painful, yes, but what did it matter?
What I was living was less than a life

But then I became a part of that story told and retold
Slightly different with each telling:
Matthew made me the occasion for an epigram
Mark tersely reported and moved past my wounding
To some boy in the crowd who ran away naked
Luke was kind enough to mention my healing
Only John bothered to supply me a name
Almost making the wounding worthwhile
I am Malchus. Call me Malchus the Small.

My betters tell me those weren't the names
Of the actual writers at all but that others wrote
Using those names for polemics and preaching
And that Malchus wasn't my name either
But a cryptic word with forgotten meaning
Such things are beyond me.
So being an afterthought anyway
I'll hold onto what I've been given

PONTIUS PILATE

I know what it is now--Truth that is
But I will not say what I know
For fear of offending anyone

Diplomacy was paramount in my line of work
Though a bit of force deftly applied
Could help one gain one's point

In my position one had to use
All available means at one's disposal
To keep from getting crucified oneself.

The sky was still pale with dawn
When Caiaphas and his gang brought him
To the Praetorium faded stars the faint outline

Of a moon like a fingernail pressed upon wax
The East boiling over with an emerging sun
A breeze rippling my woolen cloak

As I stood there looking him over seeing
Something in his olive eyes I'd never seen
In a prisoner's before that moment

I'd seen kings before and those
Who claimed to be kings--here was a king
Whose kingdom I could be drawn to dwell in

If only I could thrust away from me
The habits demands and duties of my damned career
As it is I helped him to attain the crown he most desired

BARABBAS

When the guards came to release me I stood
In shock--I was sure they had come
To whip me then hang me on a cross

Later when I heard how the crowd chanted
My name over and over in answer to Pilate
I knew I'd been used but what did I care?

What business was it of mine that they wanted
The Nazorean the so-called King of the Jews dead?
To me it was my greatest heist. I had stolen back my life.

My life--at the most a few paltry years staying
One step ahead of the law laying low
Scraping by with what I could steal--sweet nonetheless

I could hardly resist going to see the fool
Who would die in my place. I mocked his misfortune
In the heat and flies of Golgotha. The sun started scorching us

So I was turning to go having seen and sneered
Enough and knowing it would end soon anyway
When the sky suddenly darkened. His eye caught mine

And he smiled at me faintly without regret
Recrimination or bitterness. I knew then
That it wasn't the crowd that had won my release

THE SOLDIERS

They said he was a king
He needed a crown
So we gave him one

We clothed him in purple
Made sure he received the respect
He was due gave him the stripes

Of royalty with our scourge
Hailed him with our mouths
And with our open palms

We raised him up high on his
Throne secure so he could look out
On his people and they could adore him

We diced for his garments.
Treated him to a sponge soaked
In vinegar his head slumped to one side.

Things seemed to drag on
Then orders came down from Pilate
To end it for him and the others

Swift shots with an iron rod
Shattered their leg bones
They slumped toward suffocation

When we got to him he was already gone
But for good measure one of us thrust
A spear in his side just under the rib cage

And water and blood poured out
With an uncanny rushing
Like we'd unsealed a fountain.

We stood in open-mouthed wonder
Unsure whose king we'd just killed
Hoping like hell it wasn't our own

MARY OF CLOPAS

Like the other characters cast in this story
I will go down in the annals of mystery.
To name me as one of the women

At the foot of the cross seems to shed light
And yet far from making things clear
My being placed there has spun new enigmas

My name is involved in that shell game
Of names that erupts in the scriptures
From time to time multiplying the glosses.

Who am I? This Mary or That? And just who is Clopas?
Husband or father? Vexed questions yet not exactly
The heart of the matter. What did we witness--why was I there

In the Place of the Skull to begin with
Supporting Mary my sister and more-than-sister
With the other Mary called Magdalene?

We were the Eves in this hellish Eden planted
With blasted trees tortured men hanging upon them watching
Our Adam empty himself to put new foliage on the tree of life

JOSEPH OF ARIMATHEA

One would think that people never tired
Of hearing and retelling my story
Each time with slightly different details

At least one of which was certain--
I was indeed from Arimathea fragrantly named
As if it were spelled out in myrrh and aloes

Going to Pilate seemed a small service
He was only too glad not to be burdened
With another corpse taken down from the crosses.

It was one of those services for which someone
Of my rank was especially well suited
Making funeral arrangements for a dead messiah

We buried him in a tomb newly cut from rock
Not far from the hill called The Skull--a tomb
Some say I had paid for to be my own.

The stories report that the Jews immured me
In outrage for begging Pilate for his body
But it was my own devotees who walled me up

In words about fantastic journeys bearing
The grail making my staff a flowering thorn tree
In words that rose course upon course

Till they reached the height of a castle wall
Keeping me alive with food brought by angels
Making a monument from which the dead could rise

THE STONE

You may be surprised to hear me speak
You're not used to stones talking you say for there is
Nothing stonier than a stony silence but you forget the rough

Handling that woke me to life that first day
An inside job when a thief whisked me aside with a flip
Of his finger releasing what I was meant to keep within death's vault.

Besides there are precedents for my rocky locutions
Are you not familiar with the tale of Orpheus whose grief
At death poured forth so sweetly it made stones find their tongues?

You're also surprised that stones can be scholarly?
Philosophical? Brooding quietly over dusty old stories?
But I will add that Orpheus was just a type of a much greater bandit

Whose burgling from death was for a Beloved
More precious than Eurydice ever was to Orpheus
And I was there to witness the event when I failed to keep that tomb
shut up

That was long ago and all that's left of me now
Thanks to time and weather has worn to pebbles and a little dust
I'd be surprised if some specks hadn't found their way into your eyes

THE TWO ANGELS

Our question to the woman
Was to echo the one he would ask
"Why do you weep?"

For to echo him
And to anticipate him in our realm
Are one and the same thing

And the words she
Heard us say reached her
Without any vibration of her air

She would not go away
This little sister of ours
Frail in her meagre attire

Stooping her shoulders
To gawk with streaming eyes
At the place where he had reposed

Because there was no body
Just us in our radiant garments
Where she knew one had been placed

So when we asked
It wasn't to rebuke her failure
To grasp and rejoice at his victory

We merely wished to know what it's
Like to be a creature of moments
Whose heart can be wrenched to breaking

MARY MAGDALENE

I had come there before first light
The heavens still white with stars
A breeze chilled the darkness
Trembling the sycamore leaves
The dew soaking the hem of my cloak
And my feet wet in my sandals

They dried as I ran to tell the eleven
That the stone had been rolled aside
And he was no longer there

I trailed along after Peter
And the other the beloved disciple
As they hurried to see for themselves
Staying back when they left to report to the rest

Peering again I spied the angels
In purest white sitting at either end
Of the place where he had lain
 Then I sensed someone standing behind me

Why could I not recognize that face
That I had come to know so well?
You could say that I had memorized
His features as well as the lawyers
Have the sacred texts by heart

The eyes that found me without seeking
Peeling back the layers moving me
To wash his feet with tears
What made me mistake him for the gardener?

He spoke my name and I was back again
 When he told me not to touch him yet
I was relieved because as much as I longed
To embrace him again I did not know
What exactly my arms would find to hold

41

PETER

When he asked us if we would leave him too
To my own astonishment I found the wherewithal
To stand there and without hesitation proclaim

That he and he alone possessed the words of eternal life.
In spite of the crowd's defection we still
Felt invincible and what a privilege to stand

With him when the others began leaving
In droves when the loaves and fishes took on
A sour taste seasoned by words they found unpalatable

But that was when everything seemed possible
And some of the defectors even returned
After the news of Lazarus' raising spread

I was confident our boat would weather any storm.
With our master piloting us I never really looked for storms
Then panicked when the perfect storm arrived.

My absurd attempt to save him with a sword accomplished
Nothing but the maiming of one no worse than myself
And my denials met with the mockery of the crowing cock.

I tried to make amends by rushing to the tomb
That Mary said was empty but my young friend's legs
Proved nimbler than mine worn down by years of fishing.

In the end he made me the butt of his divinest joke
When he demanded that this fisherman become keeper of his sheep
Moments after making the biggest catch of my entire life

THE BELOVED DISCIPLE

You ask me how I came to be called
The disciple he loved? The answer is simple.
It was because I listened to his words and kept them.

Many wonder these days if I am
The one whose testimony is set down in writing
If I'm the one called John the Evangelist

And whether I wrote the three letters
Or had those visions in the cave
Stringing them together into Revelation.

It's not a question so easily answered.
Being an Author sometimes has more to it
Than holding a pen stroking letters on parchment.

It has to do also with seeing and hearing
And finding one's place thereby in the legends
Whether it's being the first to proclaim him

There on the seashore or reposing on his breast
As we ate the supper or seeing the lance pierce him
After being bequeathed as a son to his mother

Or outracing Peter in the whitening dawn
Then letting him enter the empty tomb first
Nonetheless spying the cloths neatly laid to the side.

I am the one who hears his words and keeps them
I am the beloved and the testimony is mine
And my testimony is true.

11576309R00028

Made in the USA
Middletown, DE
14 November 2018